SHOW·ME·BOOKS

Catch that Mouse!

A STORY IN RHYME WITH THINGS TO FIND

BY MARCIA LEONARD
PICTURES BY DIANE PALMISCIANO

A BANTAM LITTLE ROOSTER BOOK
TORONTO · NEW YORK · LONDON · SYDNEY · AUCKLAND

To the memory of my Uncle John
—D.P.

For my Dutch family
—M.L.

CATCH THAT MOUSE!

A Bantam Book / November 1988

Produced by Small Packages, Inc.

"Bantam Little Rooster" is a trademark of Bantam Books.

Library of Congress Cataloging-in-Publication Data

Leonard, Marcia.
  Catch that mouse!

  (Show me books)
  Summary: A rhyming text follows a cat chasing a
mouse through the house and asks the reader to point out
or find various things in the illustrations.
  [1. Cats—Fiction. 2. Mice—Fiction.   3. Literary
recreations. 4. Stories in rhyme] I. Palmisciano,
Diane, ill. II. Title. III. Series: Leonard, Marcia.
Show me books.
PZ8.3.L54925Cat 1988   [E]   88-3408
ISBN 0-553-05425-2

Published simultaneously in the United States and Canada

Bantam Books are published by Bantam Books, a division of Bantam
Doubleday Dell Publishing Group, Inc. Its trademark, consisting of the
words "Bantam Books" and the portrayal of a rooster, is Registered in U.S.
Patent and Trademark Office and in other countries. Marca Registrada.
Bantam Books, 666 Fifth Avenue, New York, New York 10103.

PRINTED IN THE UNITED STATES OF AMERICA

RM   0 9 8 7 6 5 4 3 2 1

This is the tale of a cat and a mouse,
who race up and downstairs and all through a house.
The rhymes in this book will tell of their spree
and ask you about all the things that you see.

There goes the mouse—so sure of himself!
He runs from his mousehole and crosses the shelf.
The cat follows him, without much success.
He knocks over everything. My, what a mess!

Catch that mouse!

Look at this picture and find the mousehole,
a bag of potatoes, a big wooden bowl.
Then point to some jars with lids screwed on tight,
a mop and a broom and the switch for the light.

What else can you show me?

Out in the kitchen, Mom washes a pot.
But does the mouse hide?
Oh no, he does not!
He crosses the sink at a place that is thin.
The cat does the same—only *he* tumbles in!

Oh, that mouse!

Look at this picture and count what you see:
one teapot, two spoons, and three cups for the tea.
Count four frying pans that hang on the wall,
five plates that are big and five more that are small.

What else can you count?

At the piano, Kate lifts up her feet,
when mouse and cat scamper right under her seat.
As you might have guessed, the poor girl is vexed.
But they just run on. Where will they go next?

Follow that mouse!

Look at this picture and find something tall
that goes *tick tock tick* and stands near the wall.
Find one thing that toots and one thing that rings,
and one that makes noise when you strum on its strings.

What else makes noise?

Here is the living room. Shhh, Dad's asleep,
even though mouse and cat race in and leap
over his paper and run 'round the chairs,
through the front hallway and right up the stairs.

Chase that mouse!

Look at this picture and show me a fish,
a bird in a cage, and a plant in a dish.
What fills up the shelves? What lies on the floor?
What covers the windows? What hangs on the door?

What other things can you name?

In the front bedroom, the twins are at play,
having some fun at the end of the day.
They're quite surprised when the mouse races in,
but they don't shout EEEK!, they just giggle and grin.

That silly mouse!

Look at this picture and what do you see?
A monkey? A clock? A small wooden tree?
Show me two bears and a shirt on a hook,
a puzzle, a ball, and a big open book.

What else do you see?

Next door in his room, Jim's painting a scene
(a deer in a meadow of yellow and green),
when those two dash in and cross his wet page,
leaving footprints behind—and Jim in a rage!

Stop that mouse!

Look at this picture and find something red.
Then find something white that sits on the bed.
What's blue in this room?
What's pink and what's brown?
What color's the suit and the hat on the clown?

What other colors do you see?

Out to the hallway the mouse and cat race,
then back down the stairs at a furious pace.
Poor Jim, Kate, and Mom don't know what to do!
The twins just keep laughing
  —and Dad sleeps right through!

Get that mouse!

Look at this picture, look left and look right.
Then let me know what each person holds tight.
Find an umbrella, two coats, and a hat,
some dirty old boots, and a clean welcome mat.

What else can you find?

Back in the pantry, all snug in his nest,
the mouse settles down to a well-deserved rest.
The cat will rest, too, at least till next time,
so there ends the chase—and here ends the rhyme.